ANSIT

4455

MW00998536

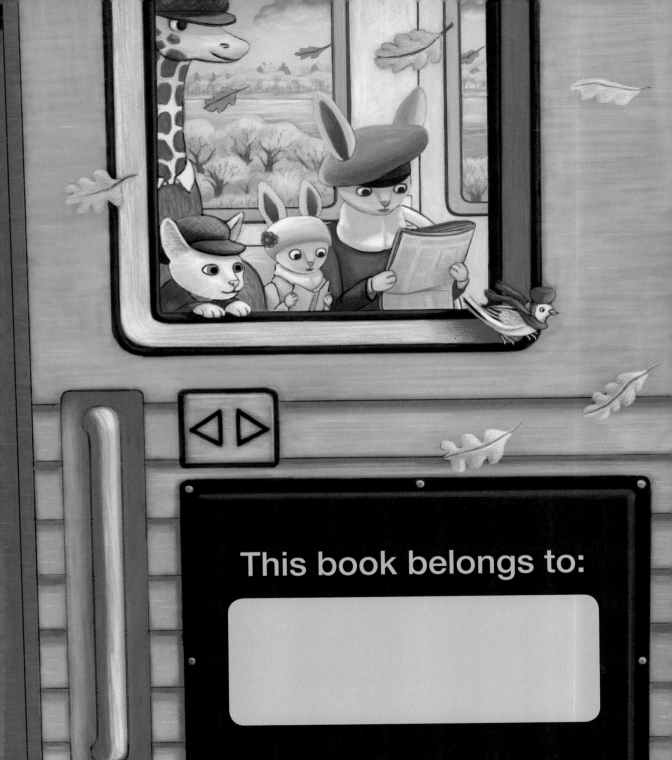

This book belongs to:

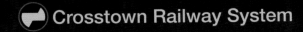
Crosstown Railway System

written by

Patrick T. McBriarty

illustrated by

Johanna H. Kim

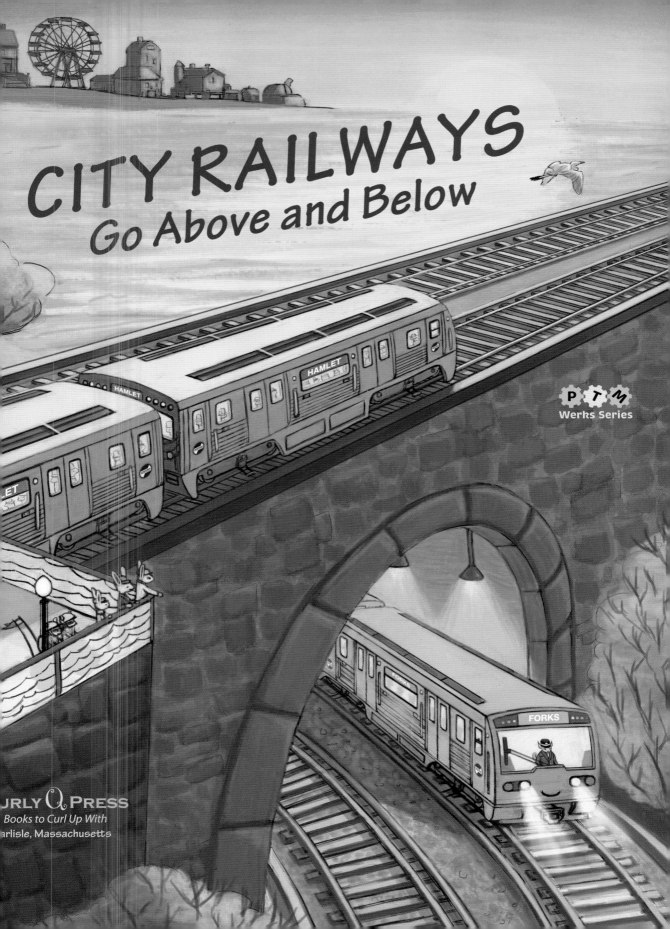

"Mom, the train yard is so big!" Ben says. "How do you know which train is yours?"

"Supervisor Rory will tell us," his mom says as they walk toward the Train Room.

"Top of the morning, Train Operator Julia," says Supervisor Rory, handing her a route assignment.

"Thanks, Rory," Operator Julia says. "Meet my son, Ben. He is riding along with me today."

"Top of the morning, Ben!" Rory says. "Be sure to listen to your ma. She's our top operator."

Operator Julia and Ben begin by checking the train to make sure everything is ready to go.

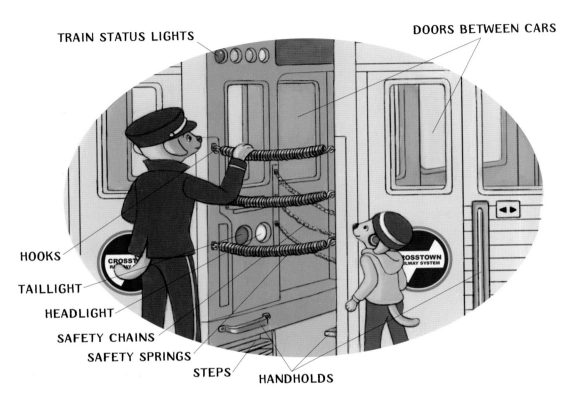

TRAIN STATUS LIGHTS

DOORS BETWEEN CARS

HOOKS

TAILLIGHT

HEADLIGHT

SAFETY CHAINS

SAFETY SPRINGS

STEPS

HANDHOLDS

HANGING STRAPS FOR STANDING PASSENGERS

GRAB BARS AND POLES

Inside the motor cab, Operator Julia inserts her operator's key *ka-lunk,* dials up the run number *clicket-et-e-click-click,* sets the destination signs *rurr-rurr-rurp,* turns the headlights and taillights on *click click,* and tests the windshield wipers *gromp, gromp, gromp.*

Last she flips the Right Door switch *click,* and *shee-opp* the doors facing the platform open to let waiting passengers *tromp-clomp-clomp* on board.

Train operators follow seven steps to go from station to station.

STEP 1

DEPARTURE ANNOUNCEMENT. Train Operator Julia presses the ACT button *phtt,* and the loudspeakers announce, "This is Red Line Run 620 eastbound to Hamlet. All aboard."

STEP 2

CHECK AND CLOSE THE DOORS.
Operator Julia presses the DOOR button *phtt*, and the loudspeakers announce *bing-bong*, "Watch the doors; the doors are closing." She makes sure everyone is clear and flips the Right Door switch *click shee-lip*, and all the train doors along the platform close shut.

TO HAMLET

HAMLET

HAML

STEP 3 **_DRIVE THE TRAIN._** Operator Julia moves the control handle forward to go. *Voorr-RRR* hum the train motors as they begin moving along the tracks *cha-chit cha-chit,* gain speed *tha-that tha-that,* and *voo-rrooMM* east toward the next stop.

As the train *voo-rrooMMs* along the elevated railway *tha-that tha-that,* Ben has a great view of the tracks ahead and of the surrounding buildings, streets, vehicles, and animals.

As they approach Anthill Station...

ARRIVAL ANNOUNCEMENT. Operator Julia presses the ACT button *phtt*, and the loudspeakers announce, "Anthill is the next stop. Doors open on the right at Anthill."

STEP 6 — ***SLOW AND STOP.*** Operator Julia uses the control handle to slow *cha-chit cha-chit,* coast, and brake *siee-shush* to a stop alongside the Anthill Station platform.

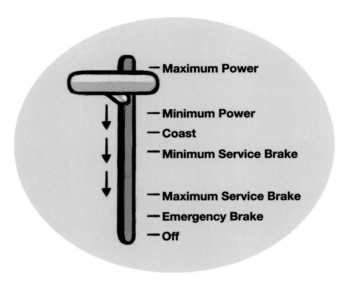

— Maximum Power

— Minimum Power
— Coast
— Minimum Service Brake

— Maximum Service Brake
— Emergency Brake
— Off

Train operators stop at the yellow numbered signs along the edge of the platform. Two-car trains stop at the "2" sign, four-car trains stop at the "4" sign, and so on. The signs are set so different-length trains may stop at the same spot.

STEP 7 **OPEN DOORS.** Operator Julia looks out the window and flips the Right Door switch. *Click shhee-opp,* and the doors open along the platform. Most passengers stay on but some exit *clomp-tromp-tromp,* and new passengers *tromp-clomp-clomp* aboard the train.

HAMLET

HAM

Train operators repeat the seven steps from station to station.

The loudspeakers announce, "Molehill is the next stop," as they *voo-rrooMM* toward the next station.

After counting the steps from one to seven for a few stops, Ben is getting bored.

"Mom, don't you get bored?" Ben asks.

"Oh, no. Everyone is depending on me to get where they are going safely," his mom replies. "A mistake or accident could hurt someone, so I pay close attention to each and every step all day long."

Ben feels the heavy train pick up speed and *voo-rroomm* along the tracks, then slow *chi-chit chi-chit* and lean into the curves, then speed up again *tha-that tha-that*. "Treehouse is the next stop. Doors open on the right at Treehouse."

Ben thinks about how his mom's job is a lot more important than he imagined.

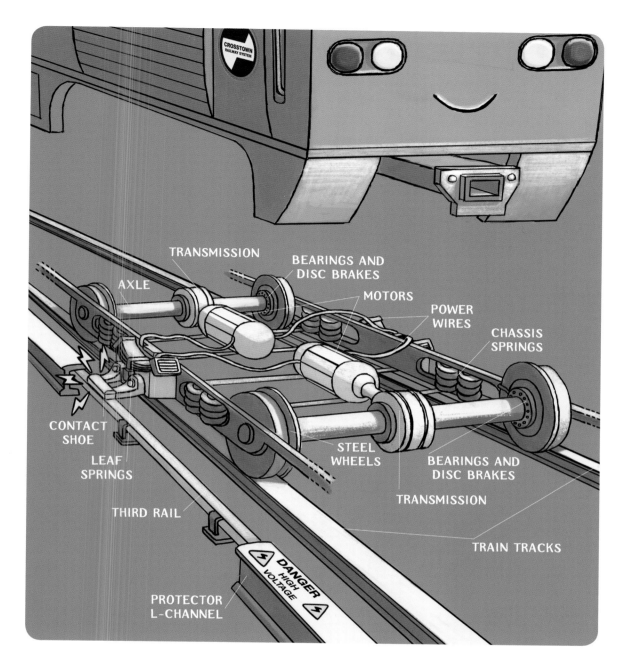

TRANSMISSION

BEARINGS AND
DISC BRAKES

AXLE

MOTORS

POWER
WIRES

CHASSIS
SPRINGS

CONTACT
SHOE

LEAF
SPRINGS

STEEL
WHEELS

BEARINGS AND
DISC BRAKES

THIRD RAIL

TRANSMISSION

TRAIN TRACKS

DANGER HIGH VOLTAGE

PROTECTOR
L-CHANNEL

CROSSTOWN
RAILWAY SYSTEM

"Mom, the train is powered by electricity, right?" Ben asks.

"You got it," Operator Julia says. "Contacts brush along the
third rail, or sometimes an overhead wire, which carries
electricity to power the train. So much energy can be
extremely dangerous. So the third rail or overhead wire
should never be touched or bumped, even by accident."

Ben notices that stop by stop, toward downtown, the train carries more and more passengers and the buildings get bigger, taller, and closer together.

"Library Hill is the next stop. Doors open on the right. Transfer to the Blue Line at Library Hill."

Ben watches oncoming trains *whoosh* by with just enough room to spare. At first he thought they might collide, but the westbound trains pass safely by *tha-that tha-that,* carrying passengers on a matching set of tracks toward Riverview Station.

Looking ahead, Ben sees the elevated tracks disappear into a tunnel. The train *swooshes* from daylight to darkness and speeds along under Crosstown's busy streets, as the headlights light the way.

"Whoa, cool," says Ben. "We just became a subway train!"

Sshh-rooming through the dark tunnels, Operator Julia stops the train at each brightly lit subway station. "Doors open on the left at Muddy Street." *Click shee-opp,* and the doors open. Most passengers stay on but some exit *clomp-tromp-tromp,* and new passengers *tromp-clomp-clomp* aboard.

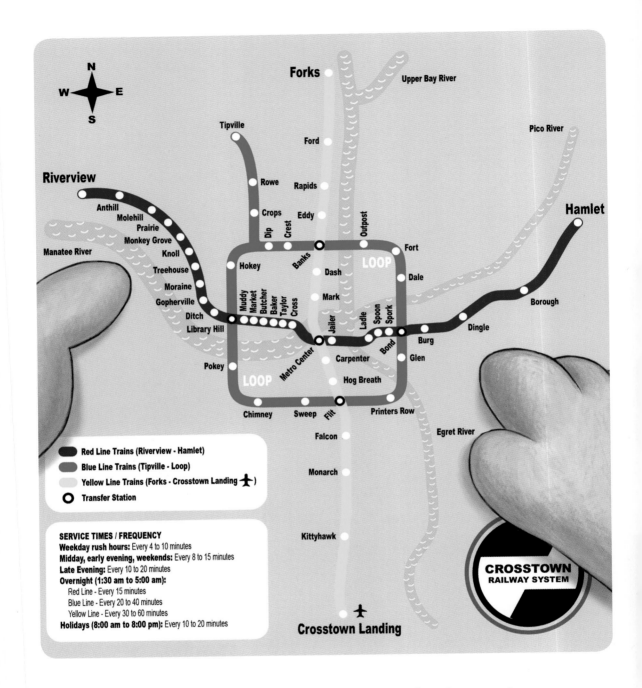

After studying the map, Ben notices the destination signs on each train display the color of the rail line and the name of the last stop to indicate what direction the train is going.

Operator Julia laughs and says, "Hold your breath; we are going under the Manatee River."

The train continues to *shh-room* through the subway tunnel. Then Ben laughs too, "Oh, Mom, the tunnel safely carries us under the water!"

"You got it," his mother says.

The loudspeakers announce, "Metro Center at Grand Hall is the next stop. Doors open on the left. Transfer to the Yellow Line, high-speed trains, trams, and buses at Metro Center."

Operator Julia says, "Do you know where we are?"

"Yes! We are under the Grand Hall, where passengers connect with the trains, buses, and trams. We visited it last summer," says Ben.

Several stops later, Ben spies daylight ahead.
The tracks slope upward, and they change from
a subway train back into an elevated train.

"Whoa, cool!" Ben says.

As they continue on, Ben notices each train station is different, but each has the same Crosstown Railway signs, colors, and passenger platforms, with an attendant on duty.

Bing-bong. "Watch the doors; the doors are closing." And they are off again to the next stop.

"Hang on," Operator Julia says and pulls the control handle all the way back. The brakes sing *sii-eee siiee-shush* and they come to a quick stop at a red signal light. She explains, "Green means, 'Go; clear ahead.' Yellow means, 'Slow; proceed with caution.' And red means, 'Stop and wait.'"

203

— Maximum Power

— Minimum Power
— Coast
— Minimum Service Brake

— Maximum Service Brake
— Emergency Brake
— Off

Operator Julia calls on her radio, "Hello, Control, (CRACKLE) this is Red Line Run 620 eastbound at signal 203. I have a red signal light but see no problem or trains ahead (CRACKLE)."

Controller Audrey replies, "There are workers on the tracks up ahead (CRACKLE). Please wait for a yellow or green signal, and proceed with caution."

In the Railway Control Room, controllers make sure the automatic signal lights that speed or slow trains keep the whole system running smoothly. They also organize repairs to the tracks and trains, handle unexpected breakdowns, and keep everything moving.

Using the intercom, Operator Julia announces to the passengers, "Sorry for the delay—there are track repairs ahead. We will be moving again shortly. Thank you for your patience."

Passengers who are in a hurry grumble, some look around, and others continue reading or quietly talking with each other.

Next stop: Borough

Ben sees the signal change from red to yellow. They begin moving again *voorr-RRR* and slowly pass through several groups of workers along the tracks *cha-chit cha-chit*.

Ben smiles and waves at the workers.

Soon they arrive at the end of the line. "This is Hamlet, as far as this train goes. All passengers must leave the train." The doors open and all passengers *clomp-tromp-tromp* off the train.

"Now what?" asks Ben.

Operator Julia turns off the taillights and headlights *click click* and pulls her operator's key *ca-link*. "Follow me," she says as they exit the train.

They walk to the other end of the train and enter the motor cab. Operator Julia inserts her operator's key *ka-lunk*, sets the destination sign *rurr-rurr-rurp* to Riverview, and turns on the headlights and taillights *click click*. "Ready to go west back to Riverview Station?" she says.

"You are going to drive the train backwards?" Ben asks.

"Well, now this is the front of the train," Operator Julia says.

Elevated and subway trains are made by coupling together two or more train cars. Almost every train of 2, 4, 6, or more cars has a motor cab at either end so it can be driven in either direction.

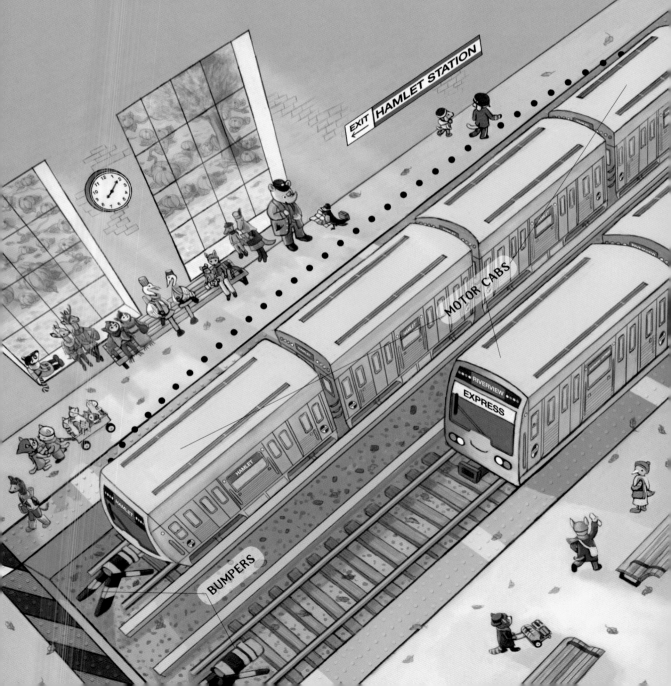

EXIT HAMLET STATION

MOTOR CABS

RIVERVIEW

EXPRESS

BUMPERS

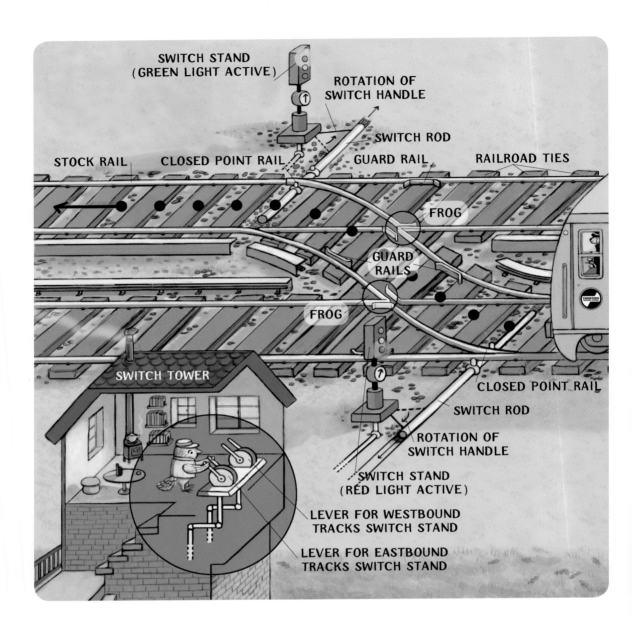

Paul in the Hamlet switch tower sets the switches so Red Line Run 620 changes from the eastbound to the westbound tracks and can continue on.

On the way to Riverview Station, the train changes from elevated to subway and back to an elevated train again.

At the end of the day, Operator Julia removes her operator's key *ca-link,* and she and Ben leave the train.

Operator Casey takes over, driving stop to stop from Riverview *chi-chit chi-chit* to Hamlet Station and back again throughout the night.

TO HAMLET

DESTINATION SIGN

DESTINATION SIGN

HAMLE

HAMLET

CROSSTOWN
RAILWAY SYSTEM

COUPLER

Each day trains move in and out of the train yard, where workers clean the inside of the cars and perform any repairs in the train barn and workshop. The big train-washing machine *spray-sprays*, *suds-scrubs*, and *spray-sprays* to clean the outside of the trains too.

Walking toward home, Ben says excitedly, "I can't wait to tell my friends all about how Crosstown Railways go above and below," and then adds, "Thanks, Mom! Uh, I mean . . . Operator Julia."

AUTHOR'S DEDICATION:
To all future train operators, engineers, controllers, and maintenance crews.
Special thanks to Graham Garfield, author Bruce G. Moffat, and Brian Steele at the CTA;
Greg Borzo, author of The Chicago 'L'; *and cartographer Dennis McClendon.*

ILLUSTRATOR'S DEDICATION:
To you, dear reader, for your curiosity about the world and kindness to animals.
Special thanks to Ernest Kim, Cate Bikales, Ellen Beier, and EZ.

Werks Series

www.PTMWerks.com

Published by CurlyQ Press
an imprint of Applewood Books, Inc.
Box 27, Carlisle, Massachusetts 01741
www.applewoodbooks.com

© 2016 Patrick T. McBriarty
© 2016 Illustrations by Johanna H. Kim

All rights reserved. No part of this book may be used or reproduced in any
manner whatsoever without the written permission of the publisher, except
in the case of brief quotations embodied in critical articles and reviews.

ISBN: 978-1-941216-14-9

Library of Congress Control Number: 2016943753

10 9 8 7 6 5 4 3 2 1

Printed in China